STRICTLY NO ELEPHANTS

Written by

LISA MANTCHEV

Illustrated by

TAEEUN YOO

SCHOLASTIC INC.

For my grandmother, Harriet, the first artist I knew
—L. M.

To Boreum, with love
—T. Y.

ISBN 978-1-338-24415-1

Text copyright © 2015 by Lisa Mantchev. Illustrations copyright © 2015 by Taeeun Yoo. All rights reserved. Published by Scholastic Inc., 557 Broadway, New York, NY 10012, by arrangement with Paula Wiseman Books, an imprint of Simon & Schuster Children's Publishing Division. SCHOLASTIC and associated logos are trademarks and/or registered trademarks of Scholastic Inc.

The publisher does not have any control over and does not assume any responsibility for author or third-party websites or their content.

13 12   21 22

Printed in the U.S.A.   40

First Scholastic printing, September 2017

Book design by Laurent Linn
The text for this book is set in Hank BT.
The illustrations for this book are rendered using linoleum block prints, pencil, and Photoshop.

The trouble with having a tiny elephant
for a pet is that you never quite fit in.

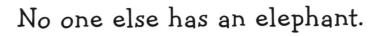

No one else has an elephant.

Every day I take my elephant for a walk.

His is a very thoughtful sort of walk.

He doesn't like the cracks in the sidewalk much.

I always go back and help him over.
That's what friends do: lift each other over the cracks.

Today I'm walking my tiny elephant to Number 17. It's Pet Club Day and everyone will be there.

"Come along. There's a good boy."

I coax him the last few feet. "It'll be fine."

When I look up, there's
a sign on the door.

My tiny elephant leads me back to the
sidewalk, never minding the cracks.

That's what friends do:
brave the scary things for you.

"Did you try to go to the Pet Club meeting too?"
the girl asks.
"Yes," I say. "But they don't allow elephants."

"The sign didn't mention skunks," the girl says,
"but they don't want us to play with them either."
"They don't know any better," I tell her.

"He doesn't stink," the girl adds.
"No, he doesn't," I agree. "What if
we start our own club?"

"Come along," I say, making certain that my tiny elephant follows me. Because that's what friends do: never leave anyone behind.

"We can play here," one of our new friends says.

"All of us."

So we paint our own sign.

My tiny elephant will give you
directions if you need them.

Because that's what friends do.